FOUL PLAY

Originally published under the title
One Cold Armpit

Karen Edwards

Illustrated by
Bojan Redzic

Scholastic Canada Ltd.
Toronto New York London Auckland Sydney
Mexico City New Delhi Hong Kong Buenos Aires

For my wonderful parents, Norm and
Elenore Brosinsky, who taught me to
find the good stuff.
— K. E.

Scholastic Canada Ltd.
604 King Street West, Toronto, Ontario M5V 1E1, Canada

Scholastic Inc.
557 Broadway, New York, NY 10012, USA

Scholastic Australia Pty Limited
PO Box 579, Gosford, NSW 2250, Australia

Scholastic New Zealand Limited
Private Bag 94407, Botany, Manukau 2163, New Zealand

Scholastic Children's Books
Euston House, 24 Eversholt Street, London NW1 1DB, UK

Library and Archives Canada Cataloguing in Publication
Edwards, Karen, 1963-
Foul play / by Karen Edwards ; illustrations by Bojan Redzic.
Originally published under title: One cold armpit.
ISBN 978-1-4431-1348-9
I. Redzic, Bojan II. Title: Edwards, Karen, 1963- .
One cold armpit. III. Title.
PS8609.D855F68 2012   jC813'.6   C2012-901657-8

Text copyright © 2009, 2012 by Karen Edwards
Illustrations copyright © 2012 by Bojan Redzic

6 5 4 3 2 1   Printed in Canada 121   12 13 14 15 16

Contents

Jordy

I woke up at 6:45 a.m. I usually wake up at 7:04 on the dot. I think I must be special or something because I wake up at that time almost every morning. Yesterday I told my mom that I must be some kind of superhero because I have awesome wake-up powers. She just laughed and told me to get ready for school.

By the way, I'm Jordy Jones and I'm ten. I woke up early this morning because I'm excited about school today. It's Friday and my class is going skating at the big rink downtown. I begged my mom to be a volunteer driver and she agreed.

Mom is bringing hot chocolate in a big thermos and she bought little marshmallows for us too.

Another good thing is that I'm getting a new winter jacket tomorrow. My old one is really gross. It's yellowy green and has poo-coloured stripes. It was my brother's before it was mine. Not only is it ugly, but it's also cold because there's a hole in the armpit where I ripped it swinging on the monkey bars. I've worn it for two winters and Mom said that it's time for a new one. Finally!

I know exactly which coat I'm going to get. It's blue with two silvery stripes around the sleeves. It has a blue and white swirly rubber zipper pull too. Mom says it's a bit expensive, but I'll be able to wear it for a couple of years, so it'll be worth it.

While I was lying in bed, I noticed that Mr. Johnson's Christmas lights were off. He usually leaves them on overnight. Mr. Johnson lives across the street from us. Every year he puts something new in his light display. This year it's a Santa in his sleigh and a reindeer with a brightly lit red nose. He put them on his roof and I can usually see the lights in the mirror on my dresser.

I hurried downstairs for breakfast. My older brother, Marty, was standing in the kitchen eating cereal out of the box. He's sixteen and just got his driver's licence, though Mom and Dad haven't let him drive anywhere by himself yet.

"Hey, brat, go get the newspaper, will you?" he said to me. "I want to see if there are any good cars in the classifieds." He tossed a few more Cheerios into his mouth.

I wanted to read the comics anyway, so I decided to get the newspaper from the mailbox.

I opened the door and a weird feeling came over me. It was so early, but there were lots of people outside walking and talking on the street.

I decided to go and see what all the excitement was about. It was cold, so I stepped into Dad's shoes and put my jacket on over my pyjamas.

I walked down the steps and across the yard to the sidewalk. I could see that Mr. Johnson was talking to his wife and someone else. He was waving his arms and pointing, and then he started yelling.

As I walked closer, I stepped on something hard and crunchy. When I looked down I saw a million tiny pieces of glass sparkling beneath my feet. Looking up, I noticed our car. The side mirror had been smashed off and the metal part had been thrown across the yard. The window on the passenger's side had been broken too.

My stomach felt sick and as I began to run, my dad's big shoes made me trip and fall. I got up, trying to keep the big shoes on my feet, and made it up the steps and into the house.

"Mom! Dad!" I yelled as I threw open the door. "The mirror's broken and the window's smashed!"

Mom came down the stairs quickly when she heard me. "What's broken?"

"The mirror and the window!" I screamed again.

Dad and Marty were now standing beside her and they all looked at me like I was a bit crazy. After all, I was standing there in my dad's shoes with my winter jacket over my pyjamas.

"Slow down and tell us what you're yelling about," Mom said.

I took a deep breath and tried to calm down.

Then Mom gasped. "What happened to your knee?"

I looked down at my leg. "AHHHHH, I'm bleeding, I'm bleeeeeeding!" I screamed. I pulled the left leg of my pyjamas up over my knee. I must have scraped it when I

6

tripped. It was oozing blood. Mom ran up to the bathroom and came down carrying a wet cloth, a cotton ball and a Band-Aid. She wiped the blood off my knee, then dabbed some antiseptic on it.

"Gee, that is a deep cut. How did it happen?" she asked as she ripped open the Band-Aid package.

"I must have cut it on the broken glass," I said, remembering about the window and the mirror.

"Broken glass? What broken glass?" Mom gasped again.

I started to tell my parents about the car, but before I could finish they had thrown on their jackets and shoes. They sprinted out the door with my brother and me following right behind.

"Watch out for the glass on the ground!" I warned them.

Vandals!

I followed Mom and Dad as they walked carefully out to the car. They looked alarmed. Some of the other neighbours who were out on the street started coming over to where we were standing.

"This is some mess, huh?" said Mr. Johnson. His face was red and there was sweat on his upper lip.

"What happened?" my mom asked, sounding sad.

"Some gang of punks must have vandalized the whole block. They pulled down most of my Christmas lights and the new Santa and sleigh," Mr. Johnson said. He sounded angry.

Our other neighbours were wandering around inspecting their cars. Most of their windows had been smashed and some had graffiti spray-painted on their cars. Some of them looked like they were trying not to cry. I felt like crying and I could see that Mom and Dad were very upset.

My brother was really quiet and just went into the house. He came out with a broom and garbage bag and started sweeping up the broken glass. Everybody was walking around looking at the damage, saying things like, "I can't believe it," and "Who would do something like this?"

After we cleaned up the glass, we went back inside. Dad phoned the police and told them what had happened. The police told him there had been a lot of destruction last night.

Dad said they would be sending a police cruiser out as soon as they could.

"I'll have to call Blair's mom and see if she can drive you kids to the skating rink today," Mom said as she reached for the phone.

"Mom, you promised that you were going to take us," I said.

"I'm sorry, Jordy, but the window and mirror are broken and I can't use the car until it gets fixed. It's not safe and it would be very chilly with cold air blowing through that missing window."

"Awww, Mom, it'll be okay. We'll have our winter jackets on. We'll be warm enough," I begged.

I knew she was right, but I had been looking forward to this for two weeks and now my plans had been ruined. Not only that, but my knee was really hurting and it had bled through the Band-Aid. This was not turning out to be the best Friday I had ever had.

Picking Up the Pieces

Mom told me to go and get ready for school. She and Dad sat at the kitchen table and talked. They sounded very serious. Dad said it would probably cost about three or four hundred dollars to fix the car. That sounded like a lot for just a mirror and window.

I didn't feel like going to school now. Why? Why would somebody break something on purpose? Who would want to ruin my Friday?

I remember how bad I felt when I

accidentally broke my mom's favourite coffee mug. It was the one that Grandma had given her for her birthday a long time ago. It had a picture of a cute puppy just like the one Mom had when she was a little girl.

Mom was really sad when I broke the mug, but she tried not to show it because she knew how bad I felt. She told me she knew it was an accident, but that I should try to be more careful. I started to cry because I felt so bad.

So . . . why would someone purposely break our car window and mirror and Mr. Johnson's lights and everything else? I don't get it.

"Jordy! Hurry up. You'll have to walk to school," Mom was yelling to me.

Now she couldn't drive me to school either. This day just kept getting worse.

As I was putting my ugly winter jacket on, Mom came and gave me a hug. She asked me if I was okay. I told her I was sad our car got wrecked. She said that she was kind of sad about it too. We had another hug and then she said, "Well, see you later, frog boy."

"See you later, tadpole." Usually I try to think of something really funny to say back to her, but today this was the best I could do.

I walked down the steps of our house and I could still see a few tiny pieces of sparkling glass lying on the ground beside our car. Mr. Johnson was cleaning up his yard and gathering up the strings of broken lights that were strewn all over. He looked up at me.

"Well, I can't put them back up now. I'm not getting up on the ladder with all this ice and snow around. You know, I don't even think I can fix the new Santa and Rudolph," he said in a mad voice.

"That's too bad," I said kind of quietly. "I really liked them. I liked the way they shone in through my bedroom window at night."

"Yes, it is too bad that some people have no respect for others," he said as he turned and started cleaning up his lights again.

I kept walking. As I got to the end of the block, I passed the lady who lives in the yellow house on the corner. She was bending over one of the Christmas elves on her lawn.

As I got closer, I saw it was broken. Actually all four of her elves were. She was carefully picking up the pieces and putting them in a green garbage bag. She looked up at me and I could see that there were tears in her eyes. I didn't know what to say, so I just gave her an "it's too bad" kind of smile.

Now I really felt like crying. I wanted to stop and help her, but I was already going to be late for school even if I hurried.

I started to run and some tears fell down the front of my ugly winter jacket. The cool breeze felt good on my face and dried the tears quickly.

I got to school just as the bell rang. Inside, several of my classmates crowded around my locker as I put my ugly jacket away.

"Hey, what happened?" Blair asked. "My mom is driving to skating because your mom told her your car wasn't working."

Everyone's eyes were on me.

"Some jerks trashed our whole block," I said.

"Mr. Johnson's Christmas lights are broken and lots of people's cars got damaged. They broke the window and snapped the mirror off ours."

"Did they catch the guys who did it?" Blair asked.

"I don't know," I said. I hadn't even thought about that yet. Maybe they were in jail right now. I hoped so.

Our teacher, Mrs. Borson, came out of our classroom and told us to quiet down and get to our desks. Once we settled, she sat on her desk at the front of the room.

"I heard some disturbing news this morning. Does anyone want to talk about it?"

Lots of people put up their hands.

"We have about fifteen minutes before we leave for the skating rink," she said.

"I saw some graffiti on the school by the grade three door," Ami said.

"Me too," came a chorus of other kids' voices.

18

"Jordy's car got the window smashed," Aaron piped in.

Mrs. Borson looked at me. "Is that so, Jordy?"

"Yes," I said. "That's why Blair's mom is driving to skating instead of my mom."

"Oh, that's a shame." She turned to me. "I can't imagine why someone would do these kinds of things. I hope they catch them soon.

"Maybe we should get ready to go. The kids who were going in Jordy's car are now going in Blair's. Meet out in front of the school in two minutes. Make sure you all have your skates. Go!" She clapped her hands and we all headed for the door.

Ice Time

Aaron, Blair, Ryan and I piled into Blair's car. Aaron is my and Blair's good buddy. We have been on the same hockey team since we were three years old. Ryan is a new kid. He seems nice enough.

When I got into the back of Blair's car, his mom told me how sorry she was that our car had been damaged. "Your mom brought over the hot chocolate and marshmallows though, so it's not a total loss." She smiled.

"Hey, Jordy, where's your new jacket?" Aaron poked me.

"I'm getting it right after our hockey game tomorrow morning!" I smiled.

"What team are you playing against?" asked Ryan.

"I think it's the Phantoms," Blair replied.

"Hey — that's my team." Ryan smiled. "Prepare to get creamed!"

"You'll be creamed corn," Blair shot back. "Go, Bears, go!"

We all laughed. Our team has been called the Bears since we were little. In kindergarten, our uniforms had teddy bears on them, but now they have big, scary grizzly bears.

The car pulled up to the skating rink. We all got out and started putting our skates on. I'm pretty fast at tying my skates, so I was the first one on the ice.

I skated back and forth waiting for Aaron and Blair to get their skates on. Annie stepped onto the ice. She fell on her butt two seconds later. I tried not to laugh, but when she looked up at me, we both started giggling and couldn't stop. I offered to help her up and then we both landed on the ice. She's a crummy skater, but put a soccer ball at her feet and she looks like a pro.

"Maybe I'd better just hang onto the sides for a while," she said.

Blair, Ryan and Aaron skated over to me and we played tag and crack the whip. It was

a blast! The hot chocolate was good too. I had tons of marshmallows in mine. In fact, I think I had more marshmallows than hot chocolate.

The rest of the day was just normal. I kept thinking about the vandals though, wondering if the police had caught them.

Walking home after school I wondered what I would see. Would the damage be cleaned up? Would our car be fixed?

As I got closer, I spotted the yellow house on the corner. There were still two of the broken Christmas elves lying in the front yard. I couldn't see the old lady. She was pretty old and maybe she got tired from picking up the pieces. The green bag was crumpled on the ground beside them. I put my backpack down and started to pick up some of the pieces and put them in the bag.

I had never looked that closely at the elves before. They were really cute. One of the elves was pretty smashed up, but the other just had its hat and one of the arms knocked off. I had a great idea!

I picked up the three pieces of the elf and ran to my house. "Mom! Where's the super glue?" I yelled as I walked in the door.

"Well, hello to you too," she said with a smirk.

"Hi . . . where's the super glue?" I said.

"In the drawer next to the sink," she answered. "Why, what are you up to?"

"I'm fixing an elf."

I got the glue and showed her the elf pieces. She put the glue on and I put the pieces in place. I remembered to be careful not to touch any of the dripping glue because I'd had a bad experience one time when I accidentally glued my foot to my skateboard (but that's another story). When we were finished, the little elf looked almost as good as new.

"I'm going to take it back now," I said, "so she doesn't think it was stolen."

I grabbed the elf and started toward her house. The old lady was out in the yard. When she saw me coming, her sad face turned happy. She put her hands on her cheeks and grinned when she saw the elf in my arms.

"I tink you be nice boy," she said with an accent.

"It just needed a little glue," I said as I put it down on the ground.

"I bring from my country when I come to live here," she said. "I keep him in the house now."

She motioned for me to pick up the elf. She opened the door to her house and I put the little guy down beside the couch.

"You are good boy." She pinched my cheek gently. "I make you cookies." She was smiling a lot now. I was too. My stomach felt funny. It was a good funny though. It felt like I was full. Not like after a whole pizza, but full of . . . I don't know, good feelings.

"I should get going now," I said. "See you." I waved as I walked away.

"Bye-bye, good boy," she called back to me.

I decided that I'd shovel her walk next time it snows. She's such a nice lady.

At supper, we talked about the day. Dad said that the police had arrested four people who they suspected of doing the damage.

"I hope they go to jail for fifty years!" I said.

"They probably won't go to jail for even one night," Dad said. "They are all teenagers, so I have no idea what will happen to them."

What? No jail! I wanted to punch them in

the nose and kick them in the shins.

"Two of them go to my high school. Everybody was talking about them today. One of them is that new kid — Kelly Marsden." Marty said with his mouth full of spaghetti. Sauce dripped down his chin.

With all that was going on, I had forgotten about the car.

"Is the car fixed?" I asked.

Mom and Dad looked at each other.

"Well, there's good news and bad news. Which do you want first?" Dad asked.

"I think I could use the good news first," I said.

"The good news is . . . the car is fixed," said Dad.

"The bad news is . . . it cost four hundred and thirty-five dollars," said Mom.

"Wow, that's a lot," said Marty. "It's not fair that you had to pay for damage that somebody else caused."

"That's for sure," said Mom. "The worst

part about it is that now your new jacket is going to have to wait a while, Jordy, and that hockey stick you needed will have to wait too, Marty." Mom looked at Dad again and they both looked upset.

"My . . . my . . . my new jacket? I have to have my new jacket. I told everybody I was getting that jacket. I need that new jacket. It's not fair! It's not fair!" I screamed and stood up. Now I really wanted to kick those guys in the shins. I was so mad I didn't want to finish my supper, even though it had tasted so good only a few minutes ago.

Mom and Dad wouldn't usually let me get away with screaming at the table like that, but today they did.

"I'm really sorry, Jordy." Mom put her hand on my shoulder. "It really isn't fair, but sometimes things don't turn out the way we want them to."

I know we're not rich, but we're not poor either. I once asked Mom how much money we have, but she said she didn't know exactly. "We have enough money to keep a roof over our heads and food on the table," she had told me.

I always know exactly how much money I have. Right now, I know there is fourteen dollars and twenty-five cents in my piggy bank upstairs. Parents are kind of funny about money sometimes.

"Nothing turned out the way I wanted it to today!" I yelled and stomped up to my room.

It wasn't fair. I could just hear everybody on Monday morning asking me where my new jacket was and there I'd be in my ugly old jacket with one cold armpit.

Pancake Breakfast

Saturday morning: 7:04 a.m. on the dot. Well at least something was going right for me. I'm still a "wake-up superhero."

I'm also still mad about the car, the Christmas lights, the elves and the jacket. But I've got a hockey game this morning, so I'll think about all that later.

I put all my gear in my bag and knocked on my parents' door. Then I heard them downstairs talking and laughing.

"Pancakes, yahoo!" Marty flew out of his room and raced to the kitchen. He has a good nose for food. I hurried downstairs too. I wanted to make sure I got some pancakes before he devoured them all.

"Hi, guys," Dad said, turning around with a pancake flipper in his hand. "Dig in."

We usually have pancakes for breakfast only on special occasions.

"Are you all ready for your game, Jordy?" Mom asked.

"Yup, all packed up." I do a checklist now because I used to forget at least one thing every game. One time I forgot my skates and had to sit on the bench and watch the game instead of playing. It was no fun at all.

"Eat up and let's get moving," said Dad. "We've got to pick Blair up and get to the game. We have to beat those Phantoms today."

Game Day

The hockey rink is one of my favourite places. It's usually noisy and cold and there are always little kids running around screaming and spilling popcorn all over.

In the dressing room I laced up my skates and listened as the coach gave us some last-minute instructions. Out on the ice Blair and I skated around to get warmed up.

"Prepare to get creamed, boys!" Ryan yelled as he skated toward us in his Phantoms uniform. He punched Blair in the arm jokingly.

"You're going to be mashed potatoes!" I laughed and pretended to mash him with my glove.

A booming voice came from the crowd, "Marsden, get your butt over here!" A tall man was screaming at Ryan.

Ryan's face turned from happy to sad.

"That's my dad," he said quietly. He turned and skated over to him.

Ryan's dad yelled at him for a minute or two and then Ryan skated back to his bench. He didn't look very happy.

The game was about to begin. The Phantoms were a tough team, but we knew we could beat them if we tried really hard. Ryan's dad screamed at him through the whole game. He had a really loud voice and it made me glad he wasn't my dad. I felt sorry for Ryan. He seemed like a pretty good player. I don't know why his dad kept yelling at him.

Both teams played hard, but with only two minutes left in the game, the score was still tied, 0–0.

Blair and I high-fived each other as we left the bench and flew out onto the ice. I got the puck and looked around to pass. Blair was right in front of the net, but there were two players guarding him. I decided to fake a pass and take it down the side. It worked! Blair got in the open and I passed it to him. He took the shot but it hit the post. Luckily, it then hit the goalie in the back of the head and bounced into the net.

"Ya! We scored!" We all yelled and screamed and jumped up and down. We won the game, 1–0.

In the dressing room, we were all laughing and joking. We were always a lot more excited after we won.

"Did you hear that loudmouth screaming during the whole game?" Matt asked.

"He was so loud, I think I'm deaf now," said

Jason, laughing and covering his ears with his hands.

Blair and I looked at each other. We both felt sorry for Ryan. We came out of our dressing room just as Ryan and his father were walking past. His dad was still yelling at him and then gave him a whack on the side of the head.

"That kid in front of the net was your responsibility!" he yelled. "If you had been doing your job, they never would have scored. If that's the way you're going to play, you might as well sit home and knit a sweater!" His voice was mean and he spat when he talked.

Ryan just looked at the floor as they walked out.

My parents were waiting for us in the lobby. We were driving Blair today because his little brother was sick and his mom couldn't come to the game.

"That was some goal," my dad joked as we

got in the car. "It was a really good game, though. Those Phantoms are a tough team. They have a new player, don't they?"

"Yes, that's Ryan Marsden. He's in my class at school. He's the new kid," I told him.

"Was that his dad screaming for the whole game?" Mom asked.

"Yes," I told her.

"You said his last name was Marsden?" Dad said looking over at Mom. "Isn't that the same name as one of the kids that got caught for all that vandalism?"

Wow, yes it was. I didn't even think about it before, but Marty had said one of the guys was a new kid.

"Do you think he might be Ryan's brother?" I asked.

"He might be," Mom said, as we pulled up in front of Blair's house.

"Do you want to come over?" Blair asked.

"Can I?" I asked.

"Sure," Mom and Dad said at the same time.

At Blair's, we watched TV, played Monopoly and took his two dogs, Rocky and Winny, for a walk. They are big German shepherds. When we were at the park, Rocky did a big, smelly poop. Blair forgot to bring a poo bag with him, so he had to pick it up in an old paper cup that he found on the ground.

It was so smelly he almost barfed. He dumped the poo-filled cup in the garbage and we decided to go back to his house before Winny did one too.

It was getting close to suppertime, so I said goodbye and started home. I walked in the house and the smell of chocolate chip cookies hit me right in the nose. MMMmmm.

"Come in the kitchen," Mom yelled to me.

I kicked off my boots and hurried into the kitchen. The old lady from the yellow house on the corner was sitting at the table with my mom.

"Hello, good boy," she said as she grabbed my hand and squeezed it.

"Hi," I said back with a smile.

"Mrs. Brundle brought you a gift." Mom pointed to the table. It was a large container of chocolate chip cookies, just like she had promised.

"I hope you don't mind, but we had one with our tea." Mom smiled. "They're the best chocolate chip cookies I've ever tasted."

As I reached for one of the cookies, Mrs. Brundle pointed at the hole in my jacket. "What happen here?" she asked.

"I ripped it on the monkey bars," I said as I took a bite. "I was going to get a new jacket today, but we had to fix our stupid car instead," I told her.

Mom flashed a disapproving look at me. I didn't care.

"The jacket I wanted was blue with silver stripes down the sides," I told her.

"You come to my house tomorrow and I fix jacket," she said examining the hole.

I said sure, but I didn't really think I'd go.

I finished up my cookie and then grabbed another as I went to hang up my coat. Mrs. Brundle followed me to the front door and put on her coat and boots.

"Those are the best chocolate chip cookies in the world," I told her as she got ready to leave. They had tons of chocolate chips and the cookie part was really soft and yummy.

"I see you tomorrow, good boy," she said as she left.

"She sure is a nice lady isn't she?" Mom said.

"Yup, and she bakes great cookies."

The New Kid

At supper that night, I was daydreaming about Monday morning and all the kids asking me where my new jacket was. "Pass the potatoes, dope," Marty interrupted.

I passed him the potatoes and then remembered about the kid who got arrested for vandalism.

"Marty, that new kid at school who got caught for vandalism — does he have a younger brother?" I asked.

"Yup, he goes to your school. Do you know him?"

"Duh, he's in my class and I played against his team in hockey this morning."

"Did you ask him what happened to his brother?" Marty asked.

"No," I said. I still felt sorry for Ryan because his dad made him feel so bad at the hockey game.

"You should tell him that because of his brother, you didn't get your new jacket and I didn't get my new hockey stick!" Marty told me.

"I think that family has enough to deal with. We should just leave them alone." Dad finished the discussion.

Mom asked me if it was okay to bring a plate of my chocolate chip cookies to the table for dessert. I said yes.

I explained to Dad and Marty about the elves and how Mom and I had fixed one and brought it back to Mrs. Brundle.

Dad was impressed — with the elf story and the cookies.

That night I went to bed with all sorts of things running through my head. Ryan's brother, no new jacket, cookies, hockey, Ryan's dad, the hole in my armpit and Rocky's big, smelly poop. It had been a full day.

snowy sunday

Sunday morning: 7:04 a.m. on the dot. Cartoons were at the top of my list of things to do today. I got up to get some breakfast and looked outside. It had snowed a whole bunch. There was enough to go tobogganing. Yahoo!

Soon everyone was awake and getting ready for church.

Vandalism was the big news at church this morning. Before church started, everyone was buzzing around discussing what had happened. During the service the minister talked about having patience and understanding for our young people. That was easy for him to say. He probably had a new winter jacket.

I couldn't wait to go tobogganing, but as we drove home from church and turned the corner to our house, I noticed that Mrs. Brundle's driveway and walkway were totally

covered in snow. I got home and put on my jacket and snow pants.

"I'm going to shovel the snow!" I yelled to anyone who was listening.

"Okay," said Mom from the kitchen.

I started with our sidewalk. It wasn't too big, so it didn't take that long. Mrs. Brundle's driveway was two cars wide. It was a big job. I had to stop a couple of times and rest. I was working so hard, I was sweating. I figured that she must not have been home, because the lights in her house weren't on.

When I was finished, the driveway looked great. I decided to go home, have some lunch and then call Blair to go tobogganing.

one Cold Armpit

Blair and I met each other at the hill. We ran to the top. There were lots of other kids. It had been a long time since we'd had snow for tobogganing, so everyone was happy to be out.

Both Blair and I have saucers. They're fast, round plastic circles that you sit on to go down the hill. They are also really light, so it's easy to pull them back up the hill.

The first race of the year was about to start. We were both ready . . . set . . .

"Hey, Jordy! Blair!"

We both looked behind us. It was Ryan. I started to smile and then I noticed it — Ryan was wearing MY new blue jacket!

I got up off my saucer and faced him as he ran over to us. He was smiling and happy and all excited, but when he saw the look on my face he stopped.

"What's the matter?" he said.

"Where'd you get that jacket?" I said.

"My mom bought it for me. Do you like it?" Ryan looked puzzled.

"Yes! I like it a lot. In fact, I liked it so much that I was going to buy it. I was going to buy it right after our hockey game yesterday, but your brother had to wreck our car and now I can't have a new jacket and I have to wear this crappy old one!" I screamed at him.

"My brother didn't wreck anything!" he yelled back to me.

"Then why was he arrested?" I yelled back.

Ryan got really quiet. "I don't know," he said. "He was just trying to make some new friends, but they turned out to be jerks."

"Yeah, sure," I said. "You're not tobogganing with us. Go find another hill."

I was so mad. He was wearing my jacket — and he didn't even need a new one. His old jacket was perfectly good and nice.

Ryan turned and walked slowly down the hill toward his house. Blair just looked at me.

"That was really mean," he finally said.

"What? Me? Mean?" I couldn't believe my ears. "Didn't you see? He was wearing my jacket!"

"Yes, but it's not his fault," said Blair. "Maybe he's telling the truth. Maybe his brother didn't do the damage. Maybe he was just hanging out with some bad people."

"Why are you on his side? I thought we were best friends," I yelled.

We were both really quiet for a while. We just stood there with our heads down, kicking the snow.

"I told my mom about Ryan's dad. How he yelled at him and whacked him in the head," Blair said. "My mom said that kids like that can really use good friends."

Oh sure, not only did Ryan have my new jacket, now he was going to have my best friend too.

"I gotta go," said Blair. He slid down the hill and started home.

So there I was . . . standing at the top of the hill in my ugly, old jacket, no friends and one cold armpit.

second Chances

I slid down the hill twice, but it just wasn't very fun without Blair, so I headed home.

"How was the hill? Crowded?" Mom asked as I was taking off my snow pants.

"Not too crowded."

"How come you're back so soon?" she asked in her sneaky Mom voice.

"Uh, well, Blair had to go home."

"Oh," she said, giving me a look that said she wanted more information.

"Ryan was there and he was wearing my new jacket." Okay . . . I'd said it.

"Oh," she said. "Did he know that was the one you wanted?"

"No, but it's not fair."

"Maybe not, but it looks like he has some problems at home and I think you should give him another chance."

"Great, now you're on his side too," I said under my breath.

"Maybe you should be on his side — I think he could use a good friend like you," Mom said and left the room.

There was too much to think about. I grabbed two cookies and plopped myself in front of the TV. There was nothing good on, so I watched a fat guy in a chef's hat make some fish soup. He left the fish heads on and everything. I was glad that I didn't have to eat at his house tonight.

Bed Head

Monday morning: 7:04 a.m. Yup, I still got it. I got dressed and went to the bathroom. I had totally freaky hair but I didn't care. One side was flat and pointing straight up and the other side looked like rats had built a nest in it while I was sleeping. I decided to leave it that way to try to keep everybody's mind off the fact that I didn't get my new jacket.

At breakfast, my mom gave me a funny look.

"Have you looked in the mirror yet?" she said with a smile.

"Yes," I told her. "It's the newest fashion. I saw it on a music video."

"Oh," she said. "What's the name of the band?"

"They're called the Rat Heads," I joked.

"It's a very . . . very . . . interesting style," she said. "I would have called them the Bed Heads."

"I need something to distract everyone at school from asking me where my new jacket is," I explained.

"I don't think the rest of the world is as concerned about that as you are," she said. "Stop worrying about it and think about the good stuff instead of dwelling on the bad stuff."

"What's the good stuff?" I asked.

"You have to find the good stuff for yourself," she told me and left the kitchen.

Easy for her to say, I thought.

The Good Things

I walked to school slowly. It wasn't cold out, so my armpit was feeling fine. I tried to think of some good stuff, but all that was coming to me was Blair and me fighting and Ryan's new jacket. Would Blair talk to me at school or was he still mad at me? Would everyone ask why Ryan was wearing my new jacket?

I heard the bell ring and I had to jog the last block to school. I got to my locker as most of the other kids were entering the classroom. I caught Blair's eye just as he was going through the door. He smiled. I smiled back. Well, that's one good thing, I thought. I felt a little better now.

I unzipped my jacket, stuffed it in my locker and scrambled to my desk. I looked up at my teacher's desk and was surprised to see a different teacher.

"Mrs. Borson had to go out of town unexpectedly, so I'll be your teacher this week," said the young woman standing at the front of the room. "My name is Miss Rogers and I expect you to behave yourselves and we will have a good time."

She looked just like a movie star. Everyone in the class was excited and whispering.

"Everyone quiet down now and get your gym shoes on. We're going to play soccer," she said with excitement.

We all ran to get our shoes and then lined up at the door to go to the gym. Miss Rogers put on her gym shoes too. They were nice white leather shoes with a red stripe down the side. She led us to the gym and seemed really excited to play. Mrs. Borson is kind of old and doesn't like gym class too much. She never joins in on the games and thinks that sports are kind of boring.

Miss Rogers asked me and Ryan to set up the goals. Then we picked teams. I was on a team with Ryan and Annie, but Blair was on the other team. It was a great game. Miss Rogers played too and she was really good. It was loads of fun and I even scored a goal.

At recess it was as if nothing had happened. No one remembered about my jacket. Blair wasn't still mad at me and Ryan and I were friends again (but he didn't have his new jacket on). Mom was right — quit worrying about the bad stuff and concentrate on the good stuff.

As I walked past Mrs. Brundle's house after school that day, she opened the door and called me to come in. I could smell cookies and ran to the door. Inside, she had a plate of cookies and a glass of juice waiting for me. I felt a little silly — like maybe she thought I was five or something — but the cookies were delicious, so I didn't mind. As soon as I took my coat off, she grabbed it from me and took it into the other room.

"I be right back. You eat cookies, Gorgy," she called as she disappeared into the hallway. When she said my name, it sounded very funny, but I didn't laugh.

I ate three cookies and drank the juice. Looking around the room, I saw lots of pictures and little ornaments. The pictures were of her children, I guessed.

"Eat more cookies and watch television!" she yelled at me from the other room.

I turned on the TV and my favourite show was on. I grabbed another cookie and sat down on a big comfy chair to watch. After a while I remembered that I hadn't told Mom where I was.

I got up and looked for the phone. It was a strange little phone beside the kitchen table. It was black and had a wheel on it. I'd seen them in movies but wasn't sure how to use it. I'd just picked up the receiver and held it up to my ear when Mrs. Brundle came out of the little room down the hall.

She was carrying my jacket — or was she? She held it up and she had sewn gold stripes on the sleeves and down the front. As I looked closer, I could see the hole under the arm was fixed too. It didn't even look like my old coat. It looked . . . great!

"Try, try!" she said, holding it up.

I put it on and looked in the big mirror by her front door.

"Wow!" I said. I couldn't believe that this was my old coat. The stripes were more like racing stripes and she had even put a new zipper pull on it. It was in the shape of a hockey skate. I turned to thank her and she had the biggest smile on her face.

"Thank you," I said. "This is even better than the coat I was going to buy. This is an original."

"You are good boy and now you have good jacket," she said as she handed me my hat. "You go home for supper now."

"Thanks again!" I yelled back as I jumped down all three steps at once.

I was running home. Mom would be worried because I always phone if I'm going to be late. She opened the door for me as I ran up the steps.

"Where have you been?" Mom screamed. She was so mad that she didn't even notice the jacket at first.

"I was at Mrs. Brundle's. She gave me cookies and fixed my jacket. See?" I said as I spun around and lifted up my arm for her to see.

She calmed down right away. "Holy cow, is that the same jacket?"

"Isn't it great? Look at the zipper pull — it's a hockey skate." I showed her.

"That is great! That's why she asked me so many questions about you the other day. She was trying to repay you for fixing the elf and shovelling her driveway." Mom looked like she was going to cry.

I hung up the jacket and admired it for a few seconds. Then I noticed the strangest thing. Hanging up in the closet was the blue jacket with the silver stripes.

"Mom, what's that doing here?"

"It was sitting on the front step just after you left for school this morning," she said. "I didn't know what to think."

I couldn't believe it. I had gone from having one crappy jacket to two great jackets in the same day. "Do you think the jacket fairy brought it?"

"Hmmmm. Not likely." She grinned. "Didn't you say that Ryan got that same jacket?"

I thought for a minute. Could he have given me the jacket after I'd been so mean to him? I guess he really needed a friend and so he gave me the jacket. Wow. What to do now?

"I guess I'd better give it back, huh?" I said.

"I think that's a good idea. He doesn't have to give you gifts to be your friend, does he?" she asked.

"No, but it was a nice thing to do anyway." I said as I put on my gold jacket and grabbed the blue one.

A New Friend

"Is Ryan home?" I asked his mom as she opened the door.

"Yes, he is. Come on in." She showed me in and then called for Ryan.

Ryan came down the stairs and looked at me. I held up the jacket and said, "This yours?"

He looked at me with a grin. "Uh, huh."

"You must have lost it on your way to school this morning," I said and winked at him.

"Thanks," he said and winked back. "Hey, when did you get the new jacket?" he said as he punched me in the arm. "It's great! I want one just like it."

"Sorry, it's the only one in the world." I smiled. Today had been a great day!